W9-BRI-573

NEW YORK

LVANIA

BORN 1774
LEOMINSTER
MASSACHUSETTS

CONNECTICUT

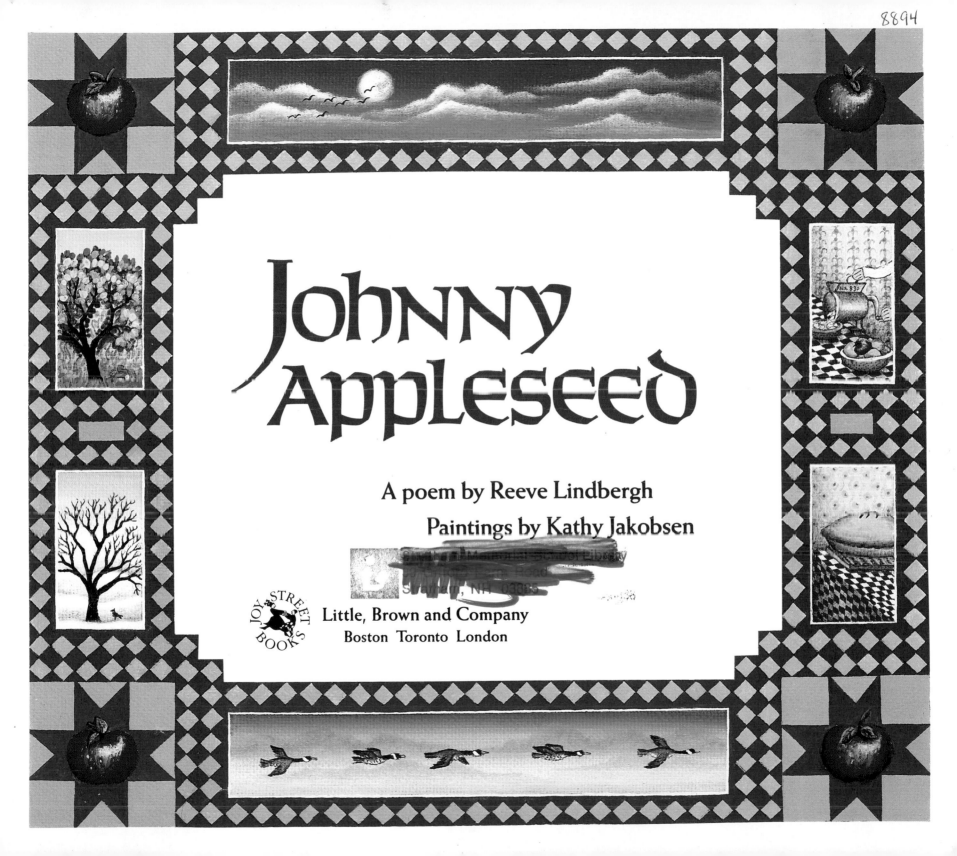

Johnny Appleseed

A poem by Reeve Lindbergh

Paintings by Kathy Jakobsen

Little, Brown and Company
Boston Toronto London

JOY STREET BOOKS

8894

Text copyright © 1990 by Reeve Lindbergh
Illustrations copyright © 1990 by Kathy Jakobsen

All rights reserved. No part of this book may be reproduced in any
form or by any electronic or mechanical means, including infor-
mation storage and retrieval systems, without permission in writing
from the publisher, except by a reviewer who may quote brief
passages in a review.

First edition

Library of Congress Cataloging-in-Publication Data
Lindbergh, Reeve.
   The legend of Johnny Appleseed/a poem by Reeve Lindbergh;
paintings by Kathy Jakobsen.
      p.   cm.
   Summary: Rhymed text and illustrations relate the life of John
Chapman, whose distribution of apple seeds and trees across the
Midwest made him a legend and left a legacy still enjoyed today.
   ISBN 0-316-52618-5
   1. Appleseed, Johnny, 1774–1845—Juvenile fiction.
[1. Appleseed, Johnny, 1774–1845—Fiction. 2. Apple growers—
Fiction. 3. Frontier and pioneer life—Fiction. 4. Stories in
rhyme.]   I. Jakobsen, Kathy, ill.   II. Title.
PZ8.3.L6148Le   1990   89-35192
[E]—dc20   CIP
                                                AC

Joy Street Books are published by
Little, Brown and Company (Inc.)

10 9 8 7 6 5 4

WOR

Published simultaneously in Canada
by Little, Brown & Company (Canada) Limited

Printed in the United States of America

For Anna, with love and apple blossoms

R. L.

To Kate, my mother, with love

K. J.

Cider mill where John Chapman collected his apple seeds

In the early days of the American frontier, when most of this nation was still wild, unsettled land, there lived a man of great courage and gentleness who traveled through the wilderness, planting apple trees. His name was John Chapman, though he came to be known to generations of Americans as "Johnny Appleseed." This is one story about his gift to our country.

These apple trees were planted here
A century ago —
A hundred years of springtime bloom,
A hundred years of snow.

A hundred apple autumns
With the wild geese flying by,
A hundred years of applesauce
And steaming apple pie.

The man who planted apple trees
Once stood here on this land,
A sack of seeds upon his back,
A Bible in his hand.

Young Hannah Goodwin saw him first,
A stranger lean and lorn;
His face was thin, his feet were bare,
His clothing old and worn.

The Goodwin family asked him in
To dine and talk awhile.
America was lonely then;
He'd traveled many a mile.

He said he'd gladly stay to sup
But could not linger here;
He had to go plant apple trees
Across the great frontier.

He said it was a wide, wild land,
A lonesome land, and long.
He said his apples, sharp and sweet,
Would make the country strong.

The family listened while he spoke
Of forests green and grand,
Of prairies vast with waving grass,
Of rivers ribbed in sand.

He spoke of families like their own,
All moving bravely west
With guns and tots and cooking pots
To claim the wilderness.

He said he'd bring them apple trees,
Our Lord's gift to the earth;
He said the sun would warm his seeds,
The rain would give them birth.

He said that each good orchard grown
Would bear fruit as God planned,
And give the yearning pioneers
A taste of Promised Land.

The Goodwin family wished him well,
And watched him leave alone.
He carried neither gun nor knife;
No weapon did he own.

For though he walked alone and lorn
Through dangerous land and wild,
He said he'd harm no creature born;
Each one was God's own child.

Young Hannah heard the tales of him
All through her growing years,
As he brought apples, sharp and sweet,
To other pioneers.

She heard he walked through day and night
And through the winds that moan.
She heard he walked in snow and rain
That chilled him to the bone.

And where he walked she heard he gave
His blessing, softly thrown:
The scattered seeds among the weeds,
The sweet fruit wisely grown.

She heard he loved the forest land
And all its creatures, too:
Wild deer and hare, wild wolf and bear,
And every bird that flew.

She heard the Indians trusted him;
He knew the things they knew:
Which plants would heal or make a meal,
Which streams ran clear and true.

He walked all trails and heard all tales;
His orchards spread and grew,
And where he went the deep, rich scent
Of apple blossoms blew.

Stratham Memorial School Library
39 Gifford Farm Road
Stratham, NH 03885

Old Hannah Goodwin saw him last
When many years had gone.
He came in by the orchard gate
A quiet hour past dawn.

Old Hannah knew that gentle smile,
That face so long and thin.
There was a Bible in his hand;
He spoke of where he'd been.

He'd walked all through America
And all his seeds he'd sown.
He'd planted apples, sharp and sweet,
And swiftly they had grown.

There was spicy apple cider now
Out on the western plain.
There was applesauce in Iowa
And apple pie in Maine.

Apples 'cross the wide Missouri
And down the Ohio.
Sharp and sweet across the land,
They made our country grow.

Old Hannah Goodwin offered thanks
For her own trees grown so tall.
He said no thanks were owed to him:
The Lord had made them all.

"To grow a country or a tree
Takes just a planter who
Will seed and tend till in the end
The earth's best dreams come true."

He said farewell and traveled on
And did not come again,
But in this orchard, sharp and sweet,
His apples still remain.

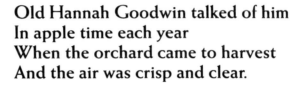

Old Hannah Goodwin talked of him
In apple time each year
When the orchard came to harvest
And the air was crisp and clear.

She'd ask children to remember
And to thank the Lord indeed
For apples sharp and apples sweet
And Johnny Appleseed.

JOHNNY APPLESEED

Johnny Appleseed was a real person, although many of the tales told about him are probably not true. People have been telling Johnny Appleseed stories for almost two hundred years, so it is sometimes hard to separate the real history of his life from the legends.

His name was John Chapman, and he was born in September 1774 in Leominster, Massachusetts, the son of Nathaniel Chapman, a farmer and carpenter who fought in the American Revolutionary War, and his wife, Elizabeth. We don't know much about John Chapman's childhood except that he probably grew up in the Connecticut Valley, but in 1797, when he was twenty-three years old, he was seen traveling west to plant his famous apple seeds in Pennsylvania, Ohio, and northern Indiana. Many people don't know this, but he even owned land in those states, and established nurseries there to raise and care for the apple trees he distributed to the settlers of the American frontier.

Apples were very important to the wilderness settlements of early America, as they were one of the few crops that could be grown and harvested easily and eaten in one form or another all year round. On the other hand, few pioneering families had room to take seedling apple trees along with all their household goods when they traveled west. John Chapman provided the answer for many people with his seeds and his nurseries. He became known by the name "Johnny Appleseed" to grateful American settlers of the early 1800s. While he did not establish all of the original apple orchards in America, as people sometimes claim, he did play an important part in bringing apples to the frontier.

John Chapman was also a devout Christian missionary who tried to explain and share his beliefs wherever he traveled. He was a follower of Emanuel Swedenborg, a Swedish philosopher who believed that we must live simply and in harmony with the natural world. John Chapman was said to have shown little interest in his personal appearance or in his possessions, but he had great love for all humanity and all living things. He gave away his trees to any families who could not afford them, and his kindness toward wild creatures, from bears to wolves to rattlesnakes to wasps, is well recorded. He was respected by the Indians and moved freely among them.

John Chapman was known to be especially fond of children. He spent much time during his travels telling his adventures to the younger members of the households he visited. He died in Fort Wayne, Indiana, in March 1845, but his story, like the apple seeds he planted, will be part of our country forever.

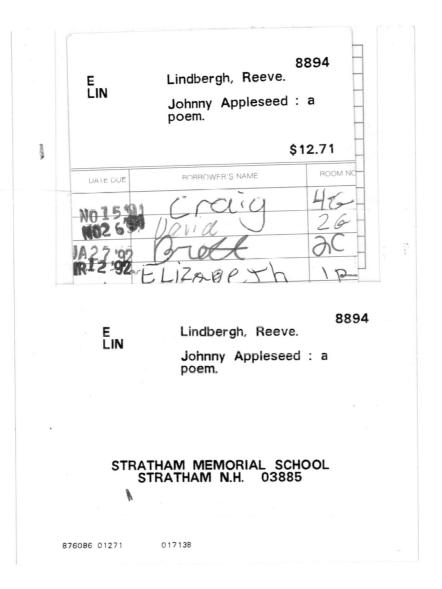

8894

E
LIN

Lindbergh, Reeve.

Johnny Appleseed : a
poem.

$12.71

DATE DUE	BORROWER'S NAME	ROOM NO
NO 15 91	Craig	4G
NO 26 91	David	2G
JA 27 92	Brett	2C
MR 12 92	ELIZABETH	1P

8894

E
LIN

Lindbergh, Reeve.

Johnny Appleseed : a
poem.

STRATHAM MEMORIAL SCHOOL
STRATHAM N.H.   03885

876086 01271   01713B